W9-ADB-207

Dusk Explorers

To my sister, Kiersty, and our neighborhood of dusk explorers.
– L. L.

To my big sisters, brothers, and cousins. For letting
the youngest one play too.
– E. R.

Dusk Explorers

Lindsay Leslie

illustrated by
Ellen Rooney

PAGE
STREET
KIDS

The sun begins to sink.
The neighborhood beckons . . .

Looking for tree climbers
who love to monkey from branch to branch
to see who can soar the highest

and find courage in the roughness of bark
and the gentle flutter of leaves.

Calling for leapfroggers who love to jump over backs
and fall down on itchy blades of freshly cut grass

and discover tunneling worms while they wait in the darkness of a tight tuck.

Searching for tag competitors
who love to sprint between huddled homes
lined with shrubs and memories

and lose track of their breath as they call
"TIME-OUT!"
right before getting caught.

Hoping for toad hunters
who love to catch hopping families
of wart-covered croaking creatures

and give them funny matching names
like Bubba, Bubbette, and Bubbarina.

Waiting for kick-the-can players
who love to run at lightning-fast speeds
to a cricket's *crick, crick, crick*

and dodge a street lamp's gradual glow
to keep from being captured.

Longing for curbside whisperers
who love to share their deepest secrets
under the soft shine of the setting sun

and snicker at the stories they dare not
share with anyone else.

Watching for hide-and-seekers
who love to duck into nooks and tuck into crannies
to keep long limbs out of sight

and wait with buzzing nerves and bat-like ears
for the moment they are found.

Wishing for firefly catchers
who love to fling their nets into the
dimming sky sprinkled with diamonds

and watch their jars glow to the soundtrack of thrumming cicadas.

Listening for giddy gigglers
who love to scream with delight at the wind
lifting their hair and tickling their noses

and pretend not to hear their parents' the-sun-is-gone yell:
"TIME TO COME HOME!"

Every summertime, screen doors open.
Porch lights turn on.

The neighborhood waits . . .

for dusk explorers.

Come!
Run free outdoors.

Steal away into the night.

Text copyright © 2020 Lindsay Leslie
Illustrations copyright © 2020 Ellen Rooney

First published in 2020 by Page Street Kids
an imprint of
Page Street Publishing Co.
27 Congress Street, Suite 105
Salem, MA 01970
www.pagestreetpublishing.com

All rights reserved. No part of this book may be reproduced or used, in any form or by any means,
electronic or mechanical, without prior permission in writing from the publisher.

Distributed by Macmillan, sales in Canada by The Canadian Manda Group

20 21 22 23 24 CCO 5 4 3 2 1

ISBN-13: 978-1-62414-871-2
ISBN-10: 1-62414-871-9

CIP data for this book is available from the Library of Congress.

This book was typeset in Cabin.
The illustrations were done with mixed media collage using paint, paper, pencil, and digital media.

Printed and bound in Shenzhen, Guangdong, China

Page Street Publishing uses only materials from suppliers who are committed
to responsible and sustainable forest management.

Page Street Publishing protects our planet by donating to nonprofits like The Trustees,
which focuses on local land conservation.